Disney's THE PRINCESSES COLLECTION
Stories from the Films

BY ANN BRAYBROOKS

ILLUSTRATED BY

KENNY THOMPKINS

JAMES GALLEGO

DEBRA JORGENSBORG

HYE COH

RAYMOND ZIBACH

PARO HOZUMI

Disney PRESS

NEW YORK

Contents

A Secret Wish

I've seen them above the surface,
  where the sun shines warm and bright.
It's hard to believe that humans are bad–
  my father just cannot be right.

Look at all the wonderful things
  they leave behind in the sea.
I can't help but think that these treasures
  were put here just for me.

I wish you could look in my secret cave
  and see what's deep inside–
All sorts of things that the humans have made
  that I cherish but have to hide.

How I long to sit on a beach
  and run a toe through the sand.
What good is my slippery tail
  for getting around on the land?

The world above is a magical place—
  I don't really mean to rebel.
But I know my father just wouldn't understand
  that I need to explore there as well.

That humans are very special
  is something I've known all along.
I hope that someday I'll have my chance
  to live where I feel I belong.

The Little Mermaid

ARIEL IN LOVE

More than any other place under the sea, Ariel loved her secret grotto. In it she kept all her human treasures, the thingamabobs and whatchamacallits that she had collected from sunken ships.

Alone, she could gaze at her trove of wonders: from the stuff that her sea gull friend, Scuttle, had identified to the mysterious objects that hummed, ticked, and glittered.

Ariel knew that her father despised humans—he had often called them fish-eating barbarians—but she was curious about their world. Ariel could not believe that a world that made such wonderful things could be bad. She wondered how it would feel to dance and leap and stroll down a street. She wished that she could spend all day in the sun, far from the rules and regulations that kept her swimming in circles under the sea.

One evening Sebastian, her father's musical conductor and adviser, had followed Ariel to the grotto, where her attention was caught by a curious object gliding overhead. It appeared to Ariel as a shadow that blocked the moonlight filtering down from the surface.

Up Ariel swam until she felt the cool air and sea spray against her face. She watched, amazed, as rainbow-colored stars exploded in the sky above. Ariel quickly swam to the ship, eager for a closer look at the humans on board.

Ariel hoisted herself up a ladder. From there she maneuvered herself to an opening where she could observe the deck undetected.

The humans were dancing!

Just then Scuttle appeared by her side. "Hey there, sweetie!" he shouted. "Quite a show, eh?"

"Be quiet. They'll hear you," Ariel whispered frantically.

"I got you, I got you," he said, winking.

Ariel noticed at once a dark-haired young man who was petting a funny four-legged creature. "I've never seen a human this close before," she said. "He's very handsome, isn't he?"

"I don't know," said Scuttle critically. "He looks kind of hairy and slobbery to me."

"Not that one!" Ariel giggled. "The other one."

Not taking her eyes off the handsome young man, Ariel listened carefully as an older, proper-looking fellow quieted the sailors. "It is now my honor and privilege," the gentleman said, "to present our esteemed Prince Eric with a very special, very expensive, very *large* birthday present."

"Grimsby, you ol' beanpole, you shouldn't have," the handsome young man said. Grimsby unveiled a huge statue of the prince. "I had hoped it would be a wedding present," Grimsby added with mild reproach. Ariel was thrilled to learn the prince was not married.

"Come on, Grim, don't start," Eric said. "Are you sore because I didn't fall for the princess of Glowerhaven?"

"It isn't me alone, Eric," Grimsby said. "The entire kingdom wants to see you settle down with the right girl."

Ariel ducked as Eric and Grimsby strolled to the railing.

"The right girl's out there somewhere," Eric said, staring out to sea. "I just haven't found her yet. But when I do. . . ."

With all the commotion of the birthday celebration, no one had noticed a storm approaching. In no time at all thunder cracked and lightning flashed across the sky. A savage wind filled the sails, and rain began to pelt the deck.

The sailors sprang to action.

"Stand fast! Secure the rigging!" shouted one sailor. The ship heaved on the rough sea. Ariel clung fast to the ropes, and Scuttle braced himself against the raging wind.

The boat pitched wildly, flinging water over the deck. During one blast, the ship's wheel spun out of control, and Eric rushed to steady it. A mighty gust of wind nearly knocked the prince off his feet. Ariel was flung crashing into the sea. She quickly raced back to the surface.

Ariel watched in horror as a bolt of lightning struck the mainsail, setting it on fire. The burning ship crashed into a rock formation, and the crew was tossed into the sea.

Ariel saw Eric bob to the surface. After helping Grimsby into a lifeboat, Eric returned to the foundering ship to save his dog, Max. Ariel watched in dismay as the doomed ship burst into flames.

Ariel desperately searched the churning water for Eric. She dove again and again. He was nowhere.

All seemed lost. Then, through the smoke and clutter, Ariel saw him! He was half submerged but clinging to some loose timber. Suddenly he lost his grip, and Ariel watched in horror as Eric, utterly exhausted, slipped from the plank into the sea. Ariel dove under the surface and, using all her strength, heaved the unconscious prince to the surface and pulled him up onshore. "Is he dead?" Ariel asked Scuttle.

Scuttle lifted one of Eric's feet and pressed it to his ear. "I can't make out a heartbeat," he said sadly.

"No, look!" Ariel cried happily. "He's breathing!" Ariel sighed. "He's so beautiful." She gently caressed the prince's cheek. How I wish I could see you smile at me, she thought tenderly. To walk with you, and—

Ariel was startled by loud barking. She saw Max bounding down the beach. Grimsby was not far behind. Someday, she thought to herself, somehow, I'll see you again. Ariel stroked Eric's cheek one last time and slipped back into the sea.

LIFE ABOVE THE SEA

*A*riel would do anything to become human, and she proved it by trading her beautiful voice to the Sea Witch, Ursula. As part of the bargain, Ariel had only three days in which to make Prince Eric fall in love with her.

Her friends Flounder and Scuttle helped her to shore. Although her new legs felt wobbly and weak, she was thrilled to feel the dry sand beneath her feet. Scuttle fashioned her a makeshift dress out of a sail, and as she was admiring her human clothes, Eric's dog came scampering down the beach.

Startled, Ariel climbed on top of a rock. Prince Eric ran up, calling, "Quiet, Max! What's gotten into you, fella?" He turned to Ariel. "Are you okay, miss? I'm sorry if this knucklehead scared you. He's harmless, really."

Ariel smiled shyly. "You seem very familiar to me," Eric said. "Have we met?"

Ariel began to speak, but no words came. She clutched her throat. "What's wrong?" Eric asked. "Can't you speak?"

Ariel sadly shook her head. The prince sighed. "Then you couldn't be who I thought you were."

Seeing Eric's disappointment, Ariel quickly began using her hands to describe the shipwreck and rescue.

"What is it? You're hurt?" he asked her. "You need help?"

Frustrated, Ariel realized that he did not understand. She gratefully accepted his offer to take her to his castle, and she was especially thankful when he slipped an arm around her and helped her walk.

At the palace Eric introduced Ariel to his housekeeper, who whisked her upstairs for a bath and gave her a beautiful gown to wear. When Ariel entered the dining room that evening, Grimsby blinked and stood up from his chair.

"Isn't she a vision?" he remarked.

Eric turned from his place at the window. "Uh, you look wonderful," he said. Ariel blushed. Eric was staring!

Grimsby suggested that Eric take their guest on a tour of the kingdom the following day.

Ariel was delighted.

Sebastian, however, could not stop worrying.

"I hope you appreciate what I go through for you, young lady," he lectured Ariel as she settled into bed that night. "We've got to make a plan to get that boy to kiss you." Ariel nodded in agreement. "Tomorrow, when he takes you on that ride, you must look your best. You've got to bat your eyes. You've got to pucker up your lips. . . ." Ariel fell asleep, dreaming of her handsome prince.

The next morning Ariel and Eric took a romantic ride in a horse-drawn carriage.

They passed through the countryside and crossed a bridge into town. Ariel could not remember a day more lovely than this.

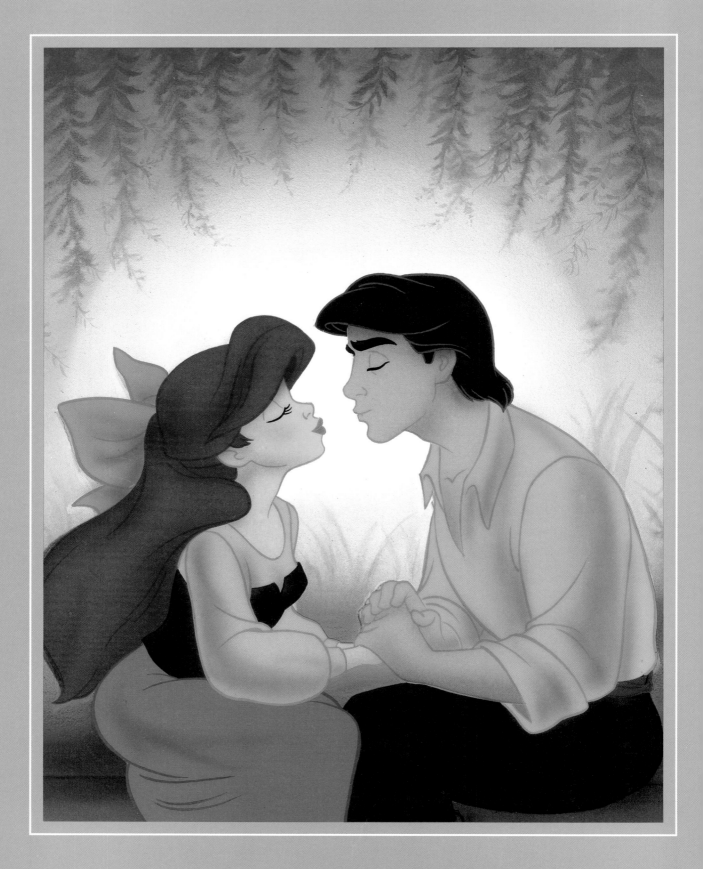

"Has he kissed her?" came Flounder's voice from the river.

"Not yet," answered Sebastian from the back of the carriage.

Still, Sebastian had to admit that things looked promising.

When the carriage clattered to a stop in the town square, Eric held Ariel's hand as he helped her down. Then he began dancing with her right there in the marketplace!

The rest of the day was just as wonderful. Eric gave Ariel a pretty straw hat, and together they gathered flowers in a meadow. After a lovely picnic, they took a leisurely drive along a wooded road.

By late afternoon the sky became streaked with pink and lavender clouds. Eric found a rowboat on the bank of a beautiful lagoon, and he and Ariel glided across the smooth water toward the setting sun.

Sebastian, meanwhile, had made it as far as the lagoon but had been unable to sneak aboard the boat. He hid in the reeds, waiting for Scuttle and Flounder. "We have to help them along," he decided. He convinced Flounder, Scuttle, and the inhabitants of the lagoon to join him in a romantic musical serenade.

The lagoon hummed with the soothing sounds of twilight. The flamingos and turtles and grasshoppers played an enchanting melody of love. Soon Ariel noticed that Eric was gazing at her intently. He closed his eyes and leaned forward. Ariel bent forward toward him. They leaned closer. Ariel felt her heart pounding like a drum. Suddenly the boat rocked from side to side, and Ariel and Eric were flung into the water.

From his hiding place in the reeds, Sebastian groaned. Ariel was disappointed, too. But she was not about to give up hope. Eric had tried to kiss her, she thought. And he *would* soon! she promised herself.

My Dream Prince

It's my birthday.
I've just turned sixteen!
But something's missing from this peaceful forest scene.

I've grown up here
with animals all around.
But still there is a love I haven't found.

My three sweet aunts
are kind as they can be.
But they don't want me to grow up and be free!

"Don't talk to strangers"
is what they always say.
But I do talk to him—each and every day!

He's make-believe,
at least for now.
But I know I'll meet my handsome prince somehow!

Sleeping Beauty

ONCE UPON A DREAM

Briar Rose knew her aunts were up to something.

Flora, Fauna, and Merryweather had been acting strangely all morning, bustling about the cottage and hushing their voices whenever she entered the room. She guessed that her aunts were making plans for her birthday, although she couldn't figure out why they were putting on such a show.

Finally, they had shoved her out of the house by asking her to pick berries—for the second time in two days! "We need lots and lots of berries," Fauna said as they pushed her out the door. "Don't hurry back," they told her, and, as always, reminded her *not to speak to strangers.*

Swinging a berry basket, Briar Rose strolled happily through the forest. She hummed to herself and gazed into the trees, hoping to meet her animal friends. In truth, they were her only friends. The cottage where she lived with her three aunts was quite far from any village, and there were few visitors.

Suddenly the sight of two birds singing merrily to one another reminded her how lonely she was.

"Oh dear," she said. "Why do they still treat me like a child?"

"Who?" cooed her friend the owl.

"Aunt Flora and Fauna and Merryweather," she said. "They never want me to meet anyone."

18

The owl and the other animals nodded sympathetically. They followed Briar Rose to the bank of a clear pool. "But you know something?" she said. "I fooled them. I have met someone!"

The owl blinked. "Who?"

Briar Rose had wandered into a clearing. The animals clustered around eagerly. "I've met a prince," she said. "He's tall and handsome and so romantic. We walk together and talk together and just before we say good-bye, he takes me in his arms . . ."

The animals gave an anxious *Yes, yes, then what?*

She sighed. "Then I wake up."

There was a great moan from the animals. Briar Rose, however, seemed cheerful despite the disappointment. "Yes, it's only in my dreams. But they say if you dream a thing more than once, it's sure to come true. And I've seen him so many times."

Not far away a real prince had tumbled from his horse into a creek. The prince took off his cloak and hung it on a branch to dry. He took off his boots, too, and left them on the bank. This gave the owl an idea. Slipping into the cloak, the owl flew back to the clearing. The rabbits climbed into the boots. Briar Rose laughed when she saw the owl and the rabbits clomping across the clearing. She clapped her hands together with delight. The animals did indeed have the appearance of her "dream" prince.

"Your Highness," Briar Rose said, and curtsied. She giggled as her prince bowed clumsily. "You know," she said, "I'm not supposed to talk to strangers. But we've met before. I walked with you once upon a dream."

She began to dance with her prince. As they twirled beneath the trees, Briar Rose closed her eyes and sang a beautiful song. She was so lost in the dance she took no notice of the stranger who approached in the clearing.

The animals saw the man, who was *really* a prince, and understood he wanted to dance with Briar Rose. So gently did the prince take her hand that she thought she was still waltzing with her friends. Only when the prince's voice joined hers in song did she open her eyes.

"Oh!" she cried in astonishment. When she tried to break free, the prince gently held on to her hand.

"I'm awfully sorry," he said. "I didn't mean to frighten you."

"It wasn't that," she said, blushing. "It's just that you're . . ."

"A stranger?"

"Yes," she said.

"But don't you remember?" The prince released her hand, and Briar Rose turned away. "We've met before," he said. "Once upon a dream."

Briar Rose turned to the prince. He took her in his arms, and they danced together, gliding through the shade and sunshine. She felt as though she were waltzing on air.

Then the two walked hand in hand to the edge of the woods. From there they looked down on the valley.

"Who are you?" the prince asked.

"Hmm?" Briar Rose replied dreamily, and then answered, "Oh, my name. Why, it's—"

She stared into his eyes and suddenly became frightened. She knew nothing about this man, this stranger from her dreams. And by speaking to him, she had disobeyed her aunts.

"No," she said, backing away. "I can't."

"But when will I see you again?" he asked.

Briar Rose began to run. "Never!" she shouted. "Never!"

The prince pleaded. "Never?"

The sound of this gentle stranger's voice was like sweet music on a summer evening. She stopped and turned. "Well, maybe someday."

"When?" the prince asked eagerly. "Tomorrow?"

Suddenly to Briar Rose it seemed that "tomorrow" was a dream that might never come again. She could not wait. She must see him again—soon! "Oh, no," she told him. "This evening!"

"Where?"

"At the cottage in the glen!" Without another word, she turned and disappeared into the forest. Tonight Briar Rose would see her prince. And this time it would be no dream.

THE MAGIC OF A KISS

Briar Rose could not remember when she had been happier. After dreaming so long of her prince, finally he had appeared that morning in a clearing in the woods. Together they had danced and walked and talked, and tonight he would be coming to the cottage in the glen.

"Aunt Flora, Fauna, Merryweather!" she called out upon entering the cottage. "Where is everybody?" Suddenly her eyes fell upon a magnificent sight. Draped across a chair was the most beautiful blue dress she had ever seen. On the table sat an enormous cake!

"Surprise! Surprise! Surprise!" her aunts sang all at once. "Happy birthday!"

Briar Rose had nearly forgotten—today was her sixteenth birthday.

"Oh, you darlings!" she exclaimed. "This *is* the happiest day of my life. Everything is so wonderful. Just wait till you meet him."

The aunts exchanged worried looks.

"Him?" asked Fauna.

"You've met a stranger?" asked Flora.

"Oh, he's not a stranger," she explained. "We've met before. Or should I say, I've seen him in my dreams."

Flora shook her head. "This is terrible!" she said.

"Why?" Briar Rose asked. "After all, I *am* sixteen."

Aunt Fauna gently took Briar Rose's hand in hers. "My dear, you're already betrothed."

"To Prince Phillip," added Fauna.

"But that's impossible! How could I marry a prince?"

Briar Rose listened in bewildered silence as her aunts explained. Exactly sixteen years ago to the day, the evil fairy Maleficent had cursed the child born to King Stefan and his queen. Before the sun set on the child's sixteenth birthday, she would prick her finger on the spindle of a spinning wheel and die. Maleficent was powerful, but the good fairies had magic of their own. The child would not die as Maleficent decreed, the good fairies promised King Stefan, but would sleep until awakened by the kiss of a true love. King Stefan ordered all the spinning wheels in the kingdom burned. To protect the child, the good fairies Flora, Fauna, and Merryweather would raise her in a cottage deep in the woods. On her sixteenth birthday Princess Aurora would be returned to the castle to be wed.

A princess? she thought in disbelief. Me? *And I'm betrothed to Prince Phillip!*

"But this can't be," she insisted. "The man I met in the forest— he's coming here tonight."

"I'm sorry, child," Flora said. "But you must never see that young man again."

23

There was nothing Briar Rose could do but weep.

That evening, under the cover of darkness, she was spirited back to the castle. She was led up a winding set of stairs to an empty chamber deep in the castle.

"Bolt the door, Merryweather," said Flora. "And Fauna, pull the drapes." Flora turned to her. "Now, dear," she said, guiding Briar Rose to a chair before a dressing table. "If you'll just sit here."

Briar Rose did as she was told. Flora then produced a magic wand. "This one last gift, dear child, for thee. The symbol of thy royalty." She peered into the mirror. "A crown to wear in grace and beauty, as is thy right and royal duty."

Suddenly it was not the face of Briar Rose in the mirror but that of Princess Aurora.

"Come," said Flora to Fauna and Merryweather. "Let her have a few minutes alone."

So it's true, she thought to herself sadly. I am a princess. No longer am I Briar Rose. No longer do I live in a small cottage in the glen. She remembered the handsome stranger she had met in the woods that morning—the man she had thought was her true love. She tried to blink back her tears. He was a dream prince, after all.

Briar Rose gazed pitifully into the empty fireplace. All at once she was overcome by the strangest sensation. As if in a dream, the fireplace transformed itself into a narrow, twisting staircase. She felt herself drawn up the stairs to a room with a spinning wheel. *Touch the spindle,* a murmuring voice called out. Obediently she touched the spindle and immediately fell into a deep sleep.

When Flora, Fauna, and Merryweather returned a short time later, they cried out in despair. How could they have left her alone! They carried the princess to a bed and draped a coverlet over her. They

must find Prince Phillip at once! they agreed. Only the kiss of a true love will awaken the princess from her slumber!

"Poor King Stefan and the queen," said Fauna.

"They'll be heartbroken when they find out," said Merryweather with a heavy sigh.

"They never will find out!" Flora decided. Merryweather and Fauna gave her a quizzical glance. Flora smiled. "We'll put them to sleep until Briar Rose awakens."

Across the entire kingdom the three good fairies flew with a magic dust that sprinkled down like a gentle rain. Soon all the inhabitants fell into a drowsy slumber. Streetlights flickered one by one and went dark. Even the fountain in the square ceased its bubbling. Not a single living soul stirred in the entire kingdom except Prince Phillip, who true to his word appeared that evening at the cottage in the glen. Instead of Briar Rose, however, he was met by Maleficent! After a valiant battle, Phillip defeated the evil Maleficent and raced to the castle. He dashed from room to room until he found the slumbering princess. He bent down and kissed her gently. Slowly her eyes opened, and Briar Rose recognized Phillip immediately as the handsome stranger she had met in the forest.

"We've met before," Phillip whispered. "Once upon a dream." With joy in her heart, Briar Rose realized this was no dream. The kiss from Phillip had broken the curse. The kiss from a heart's true love!

The kingdom awoke as if from darkness into sunshine. Princess Aurora and Prince Phillip would marry immediately and live happily ever after.

A World of Enchantment

Every morning as I make my way through town,
The people whisper to each other and look down.
Do they think I'm not aware of what they say?
"The girl is odd. All she does is read all day!"

It's true that I find pleasure in a book.
For adventure there's no better place to look.
There are princesses and castles by the sea—
And a handsome prince awaits in chapter three!

How I long to go someplace I've never been,
Far from this provincial town that I live in.
And if I can find these places when I read,
There's no telling where my dreams will really lead!

Beauty and the Beast

A PROMISE BROKEN

Belle had made a promise. If the Beast released her sick father from his castle, she would remain his prisoner . . . forever. Unhappy as she was, Belle was determined to keep her promise. It was only when the Beast flew into a rage at her for wandering into his private lair that Belle broke her promise. Belle flew from the room. "I must leave this place at once!" she cried.

Not far from the castle, however, where the road narrowed into the dark forest, Belle was attacked by a pack of vicious wolves. Suddenly the Beast appeared. He fought off the snarling wolves but was wounded and lay helpless in the snow. I could run away again, Belle thought. But the Beast saved my life. Belle knew she could not abandon him. She helped the Beast onto her horse and led him back to the castle.

The next day the Beast asked Belle to follow him. They stood outside a pair of enormous double doors. "Belle, there's something I want to show you," he said, almost shyly. "But first, you have to close your eyes. It's a surprise."

Belle frowned, not sure she should trust him. But when she saw the silly grin on his face, she closed her eyes. The doors opened, and Belle felt the Beast take her hand.

"Can I open my eyes yet?" she asked.

"No, no. Not yet," the Beast replied.

The Beast must have pulled aside some heavy drapes because Belle could suddenly feel sunlight on her face.

"Now can I open my eyes?" she begged.

"All right," he said. "Now."

Belle gasped. All around her were shelves and shelves of books. "I can't believe it!" she cried, clapping her hands together. "I've never seen so many books in all my life!"

"You . . . you like it?" the Beast asked eagerly.

"It's wonderful!" she exclaimed. Belle loved books. She adored books so much that she often read the same one twice, or even three times. When she lived with her father in the village, she had gone to the bookseller's every day. Now she was surrounded by books, hundreds and hundreds of them, stacked so high they seemed to reach up to the sky.

"Then it's all yours," said the Beast.

Belle took the Beast's paws. "Oh, thank you so much!" She was both grateful and surprised, having never expected such generosity.

With each passing day, Belle began to learn more and more wonderful things about the Beast.

One morning Belle showed the Beast how to feed the birds. When the Beast held out his paws, Belle filled them with crumbs. But the birds shied away from this imposing character, so she took some of the food and sprinkled it on the ground. One brave cardinal pecked its way up to the Beast, then leapt into his outstretched paws. The Beast grinned in delight, and Belle smiled.

The Beast spread out his arms, and the birds landed all over him. As the Beast stood there like a perplexed, eager child, Belle began to think that there was something sweet and almost kind about him.

True, he *had* been mean and rude, but now he was showing a more gentle side. Belle decided he was proving to her that he could be shy and unsure and courageous all at the same time.

The Beast smiled hopefully in her direction. Belle smiled back and was surprised at her feelings of affection. He was no Prince Charming, she knew, but he had qualities Belle was just beginning to discover. I'm enjoying myself, Belle was surprised to realize.

That evening Belle and the Beast dressed for dinner. Belle wore an elegant gown and gloves that had been woven with gold thread. She hurried out of her room and waited on the grand staircase. Soon the Beast appeared. His hair had been combed, and he looked quite handsome in an evening coat and trousers. He bowed to Belle, and she curtsied. Then he graciously took her arm and led her downstairs.

They entered a beautiful dining room. During dinner they were serenaded by an enchanted coat rack that played the violin. Belle could not help noticing with a smile that the Beast used his spoon like an expert. He must have practiced all day, Belle thought.

When dinner was over, Belle asked, "Would you like to dance?"

The Beast hesitated. "I don't know how," he replied.

"Then I'll show you. Come with me." Belle smiled and gently pushed him into the ballroom. She had been inside it only once, during the day, when the curtains were drawn. At night a million stars glittered beyond the huge windows. They seemed close enough to touch.

Belle and the Beast began to dance. The Beast was a bit awkward at first, but soon he and Belle were gliding like swans across the floor. Finally, they wandered hand in hand onto the balcony and stood without speaking under a canopy of stars. Belle remembered

the birds that morning who, cautious at first, had learned to trust the Beast. Perhaps I could learn to trust him, too, Belle thought.

After a time the Beast spoke. "Are you happy here, Belle?"

She gazed into his eyes. "Yes."

A PROMISE KEPT

To Belle it seemed an eternity before her horse, Philippe, emerged from the forest and clattered onto the drawbridge below the Beast's castle. Would she be able to save the Beast from Gaston and the angry mob from the village? Belle looked up and gasped. On the parapet the Beast lay on his back. Gaston loomed over him, a club in his hand. "No! Gaston, don't!" Belle cried out, and flew up the castle stairs to reach them. The wind whipped her hair and the rain slapped at her face as she ran out onto a balcony. "Beast!" she shouted into the darkness. "Beast!"

Finally, there came a voice that brought tears to her eyes.

"Belle," said the Beast as he limped from the darkness into the light. Belle had never been more happy to see anyone in her entire life. She wanted to throw her arms around him and cry with joy. She leaned over the balcony with her arms outstretched.

The Beast climbed up and took Belle by the hand. "You came back," he said. Belle smiled sweetly. He gently caressed her face. She closed her eyes and sank into his warm embrace.

Suddenly she felt the Beast go limp. Gaston had stabbed him in the back! Now Gaston was raising his bloody dagger for a second blow. Belle cried out and reached for the Beast, who turned to struggle with Gaston. Gaston lost his balance and plunged screaming down into the darkness.

The Beast, his strength gone, collapsed to the stone floor. Belle sank to her knees and cradled him in her arms.

"Belle, you came back."

"Of course I came back," Belle said. She laid her head upon his chest. When she felt him struggle to speak, she sat up. Her eyes were wet with tears.

"Maybe," he said, "it's better this way."

"Don't talk like that," Belle said. "You'll be all right. We're together now. Everything's going to be fine. You'll see."

Belle gently stroked his face. She spoke from her heart.

"Don't go," Belle whispered. "I love you."

The Beast closed his eyes. Thinking she had lost him forever, Belle lowered her head and wept.

All at once a strange glow came into the air. Belle watched bewildered as the rain began to sparkle and shimmer with light. The Beast was gently lifted into the air and turned as if in a slow twirling current of stars. As if by magic the Beast was transformed into a handsome prince. Belle had unknowingly freed him from a ten-year curse that was about to become permanent. The Beast had to make someone love him by the time the last petal fell from the enchanted rose. Otherwise, he would remain a Beast forever.

Just after Belle confessed her love, the last petal fell soundlessly in the castle. But the spell was broken!

Belle could hardly believe her eyes.

"Belle," the prince said reassuringly. "It's me." He smiled and stepped closer.

Belle searched the young man's face. There *is* something familiar about him, she admitted to herself. Then she gazed deep into his eyes. There was a warmth in them that spoke to Belle's heart as

clearly as words. Belle had no doubts. "It *is* you!" she cried happily. She threw herself into his arms, and they shared a long kiss.

Suddenly the gloomy castle awakened into light. The meadows all around burst into bloom. Cries of joy could be heard throughout the castle as the enchanted objects were changed back into real people.

The prince grinned and hugged each and every one of them.

Suddenly all the people in the castle found themselves in the grand ballroom, where earlier Belle had taught the Beast to dance. The prince wore the same elegant blue coat and shiny black boots as before. Belle remembered how happy she had been when he had taken her hand that evening and escorted her to dinner. Later that evening they had danced and wandered onto the balcony in the moonlight. It was then, Belle remembered, that she had first thought she might love the Beast.

Now in her beautiful golden gown, Belle danced with her gentle prince. For years Belle had dreamed of living a life of enchantment. At last her dream had come true.

A Cottage in the Woods

I don't know what his name was,
but he must have been a prince.
I met him at the well
and I've been dreaming of him since!

I had to flee the castle
for reasons still unclear;
it seems my stepmother, the queen,
can't stand to have me near.

I now live in a cottage
tucked deep into the wood.
The men that make their home there
are very kind and good.

Yet, I still hope my handsome prince
will carry me away.
And though it's just a dream I have,
perhaps he'll come today!

Snow White and the Seven Dwarfs

SNOW WHITE MEETS THE DWARFS

Snow White lived in the castle with her evil stepmother, the queen, and although the princess was forced to dress in rags and do chores, she was happy as long as she had some time alone to sing and dream. One day Snow White learned that the queen had become so terribly jealous of her that she had schemed to do away with her! Snow White decided to run away.

As the princess fled, branches tore at her clothing and bats whooshed by in a cloud of rushing wings. The whorls and knots of trees formed hideous faces. When she stumbled into a pond, the logs became leering alligators. Soon she could run no farther, and she collapsed to the ground.

Later, when Snow White awoke, a group of friendly animals led her to a quaint little cottage in a glen.

Snow White knocked on the door. When no one answered, she crept inside. "Why, there are seven little chairs!" she said. "There must be seven little children."

Seven rather messy children, Snow White thought to herself. Cobwebs hung from the corners, and dust covered everything. Right away Snow White decided to tidy up the cottage.

All day long Snow White brushed and scrubbed and swept and scoured. Upstairs she discovered seven adorable little beds.

"Look!" she said. "The beds have names carved on them!

Doc . . . Happy . . . Sneezy . . . Dopey. What funny names for children! And there's Grumpy . . . Bashful . . . and Sleepy. I *am* a little sleepy myself.'' Snow White stretched out across the beds and quickly fell fast asleep.

Snow White dreamed that seven little men had crept into the room. She thought she heard them say, ''Gosh! What a monster! It covers three beds! Let's kill it before it wakes up!'' Suddenly Snow White did wake up.

''Why, you *are* little men!'' she said, peering at the seven dwarfs at the foot of the beds. ''How do you do,'' Snow White said politely.

''How do you do *what*?'' said one dwarf, folding his arms and frowning impressively.

''You can talk!'' Snow White beamed. ''Now, don't tell me who you are. Let me guess.

''You're Doc,'' she said to the dwarf with glasses teetering on his nose.

''Uh-huh,'' Doc grinned foolishly. ''Why, yes . . . that's true!''

''And you're . . . you're Bashful.'' The little man bowed his head, blushed, and tied his beard in a knot.

When a third dwarf stretched out his arms and yawned, Snow White said, ''You're Sleepy.''

''How'd you guess?'' he mumbled drowsily. The dwarfs laughed, and Snow White sat up straighter in bed, pleased at having guessed their names right so far.

One of the dwarfs tried to hold back a sneeze, and Snow White knew instantly that he was Sneezy. When another dwarf shook all over when he laughed, he wouldn't even let her say his name. ''Happy, ma'am,'' he blurted. ''That's me.''

Then he pointed to his companion, whose silly grin was almost

as big as his huge, wiggling ears. "And this is Dopey," announced Happy. "He don't talk none."

"You mean he can't?" Snow White asked.

"He don't know," Happy declared. "He never tried!"

"Oooh," Snow White said to a serious-looking dwarf. She crossed her arms and tried to look stern. "You must be Grumpy."

"Heh!" Grumpy snorted. "We know who we are." He glared at Doc. "Ask her who *she* is and what *she's* doing here."

Doc took a nervous step forward. "What are you and who are you doing?" he asked. "I mean," he corrected himself, "*who* are you, my dear?"

"How silly of me," she said. "I'm Snow White."

"The princess?" the dwarfs asked all at once. Doc was impressed.

"Well, well," he said. "My dear Quincess. I mean, *Princess*." Doc bowed like a gentleman. "We're honored."

Snow White curtsied.

"Aw, shut up," Grumpy told Doc. He jerked a thumb at Snow White. "And tell her to get out!"

"Please don't send me away," Snow White pleaded. "If you do, she'll kill me."

The dwarfs gasped. "Kill you! Who will? Yes, who?"

"My stepmother, the queen," said Snow White.

"The queen!" they cried. Snow White nodded.

"She's wicked," said Bashful.

"She's bad," agreed Happy.

"She's bighty bean," sniffed Sneezy.

"She's an old witch!" Grumpy said. "I'm warning you, if the queen finds Snow White here, she'll sweep down and wreak her vengeance on us!"

"But she doesn't know where I am!"

"She knows everything," Grumpy said. "She's full of black magic!"

"She'll never find me here," the princess promised. "And if you let me stay, I'll keep house for you. I'll wash and sew and sweep and cook—"

"Cook!" the dwarfs shouted delightedly, stumbling over themselves.

"Can you make dapple lumpkins," Doc asked excitedly. "Uh, lumple dapplin's?"

"Apple dumplin's!" finished Sneezy and Grumpy.

Snow White smiled. "Yes, and I can make plum pudding and gooseberry pie."

"Gooseberry pie!" the dwarfs shouted in unison. "Hurray, she stays!"

A great cheer went up in the cottage. The dwarfs clapped and sang and hopped about. Snow White celebrated, too. She had made seven new friends and found a new home far away from the evil queen and her dark magic. Everyone was happy . . . even Grumpy.

A POISONED APPLE

Despite the dwarfs' warning that the queen would stop at nothing to harm her, Snow White could not help having a kind and trusting heart. So it was that one morning when the dwarfs went off to work and an old beggar woman appeared at the cottage door, Snow White did not suspect that this was the queen in disguise.

The old woman offered Snow White a delicious red apple. Snow White hesitated, then at last took a bite.

It was a poisoned apple! Snow White sank into a deathlike sleep from which only love's first kiss could awaken her. When the dwarfs returned later that day, they found Snow White slumped on the cottage floor. Overcome with grief, they built Snow White a coffin of glass and gold, but they could not bring themselves to bury the beautiful princess. Instead, they carried her to a shaded clearing of the forest, where they gathered flowers for her coffin. There, day and night, the dwarfs stayed with her.

"I'll never forget the day we met the princess and she made us wash for supper," Doc said.

"Heh!" Grumpy snorted. "And I would have stayed on the barrel and remained good and dirty if you nanny goats hadn't grabbed me and tossed me in the tub!"

Doc looked at him curiously. "You're not sorry we let her stay with us, are you?"

"Heh!" snorted Grumpy for the second time. "I knew her wiles were gonna work on us, and they did."

"But they weren't such wicked wiles, were they?" Doc asked.

Grumpy said nothing, but hung his head.

Dopey, too, was lost in his own memories. As he gathered daisies, he felt an acorn fall on his head. It reminded him of the way Snow White used to kiss him good-bye. Each time, she had grabbed his big, funny ears and kissed him on the top of his bald head.

Doc saw the miserable expressions on the dwarfs' faces. "Courage, men, courage," he said.

"That's right!" said Happy. "We must have courage. We must remember the good times, like the night we all danced with Snow White."

Bashful blushed. He had thought of that evening often. It had

started with a song, which he and Happy were supposed to sing. Happy did all right, getting through his verse perfectly, but when it was Bashful's turn, he had stuttered and giggled in front of the princess. She did not seem to mind, though, and Bashful finally calmed down enough to finish.

"I remem—," tried Sneezy, "I remem—" He held one finger under his nose and, with the other hand, put down his bouquet. Like everything else, flowers made him sneeze. His words came in a rush. "I-remember-when-Dopey-stood-on-my-shoulders-and-we-danced-with-the-princess!—*achoooo*!"

That night Dopey had climbed on top of Sneezy's shoulders so the two of them would be tall enough to dance with Snow White. Dopey's long coat hung to the floor so Sneezy could hardly see where he was going. Worse, he had trouble holding back a sneeze. When he peeked out from the folds of Dopey's coat, he was thrilled to see the princess laughing and smiling.

Sneezy struggled to keep step with Snow White. Finally, he could not stop himself from sneezing. "*Achooooo!*" Dopey toppled to the floor, and everyone laughed, including the princess.

"You sure looked funny," grinned Sleepy, smothering a yawn. "But the best thing I remember . . . about that night . . . was the story . . . the princess told us."

"It was a love story," Bashful reminded them.

"Mush!" exclaimed Grumpy. "Love stories! Got no use for 'em!"

"Once there was a princess," said Doc, "who fell in love with a prince. The prince was so romantic, the princess could not resist letting him steal a kiss."

"A kiss . . . ," sighed Bashful.

"We *know* what happens after that!" said Grumpy impatiently.

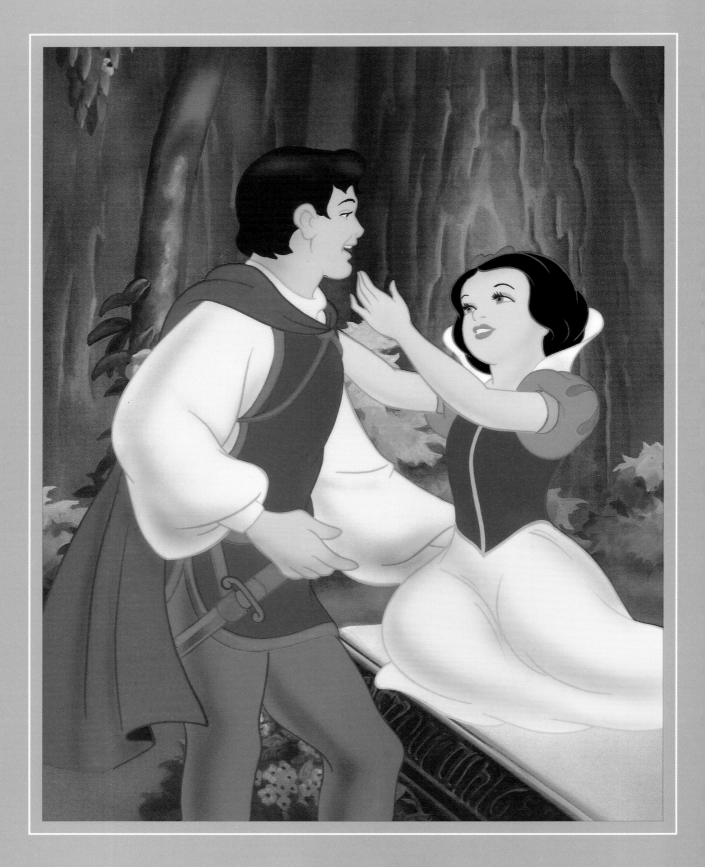

"She came to our cottage, and that old witch did away with her. Now cut out the mushy stuff!"

The dwarfs said nothing for a while. They knew Grumpy missed Snow White. Grumpy, too, had come to love her.

"I will never forget the song she sang," Happy said. "She hoped that her prince would come for her and that he would carry her away to his castle. She sang about the springtime, when their love would be renewed. She sang about the birds singing, and wedding bells ringing, and the day her dreams would come true."

One by one the dwarfs approached the glass-and-gold coffin and arranged their flowers around it. Doc and Happy lifted the glass cover and set a bouquet in Snow White's hands. Then they stepped back and kneeled. Suddenly a voice came out from the clearing, a man's voice that was strong and clear. The dwarfs watched in amazement as a tall, handsome man led his horse to Snow White's coffin. He leaned over the princess and kissed her. Then the man kneeled.

Snow White's eyes opened. When she saw the prince, she smiled. She held out her arms, and he embraced her. Then he lifted her up and carried her to his horse.

The dwarfs hugged one another and tossed their hats into the air. They cheered. They danced and sang, and the forest rang with the sounds of their happiness.

The beautiful princess and her prince prepared to leave the forest. As Snow White sat on the horse, the prince lifted up each of the dwarfs so she could kiss him farewell. "Good-bye," she said. "Good-bye!"

The dwarfs waved a final farewell as Snow White and her prince rode off toward the castle, where wedding bells would soon peal with the promise of "happily ever after."

A Dream of a Dance

I do as I'm told, I do as I must.
I sweep and I sew and I mop and I dust.

And just when I've finished with every last chore,
my stepsisters walk in and give me one more.

I live in an attic, I dress all in rags.
I never complain when my stepmother nags.

Oh, this life full of chores isn't really so bad,
though sometimes I do feel a little bit sad.

The mice and the birds cheer me up when I'm down—
they even made me a beautiful gown.

Perhaps one day I'll get to go to a ball,
then I'll be the happiest sister of all.

Cinderella

A BALL GOWN FOR CINDERELLA

In honor of His Highness, the prince, and by royal command, every eligible maiden is to attend . . .

I t had been decided the prince should marry—but first he must fall in love. Therefore, a royal ball would be held to which every eligible girl in the kingdom would be invited.

"Why, that means I can go, too!" Cinderella said.

"Well, yes. I suppose it does," her selfish stepmother, Lady Tremaine, was forced to agree. "But only if you get all your work done *and* only if you have something suitable to wear."

Tonight I will wear a beautiful flowing gown, Cinderella thought. And the prince will ask me to dance!

All day long Cinderella scrubbed and scoured and swept. She did all the laundry and mended her stepsisters' clothes. She even gave her stepmother's horrid cat, Lucifer, a bath. By the time Cinderella finished her chores it was nearly time for the ball. And, still, her dress wasn't ready!

"Oh well," Cinderella told herself as she climbed the stairs to her tiny room in the attic. "What's a royal ball? After all, I suppose it would be frightfully dull and . . . and boring. It would be . . ." Cinderella's shoulders drooped with disappointment. "It would be completely wonderful."

Cinderella was miserable. But suddenly her two friends Gus and Jaq, the chateau mice, appeared, hopping up and down and chattering in a most excited fashion.

"Surprise! Surprise!" they yelled, and pointed to a dressmaker's dummy. There stood a beautiful party gown! It was pink, with white ruffles and a silk sash. Near the dress lay a necklace of perfect blue beads.

"Why, I never dreamed—," Cinderella exclaimed. "How can I ever . . . Why, thank you so much!" Cinderella would go to the ball after all!

"Mother!" whined Drizella and Anastasia when Cinderella appeared, radiant in her gown. "She can't go! You can't let her go!"

"Girls, please!" cried Lady Tremaine.

"After all, I did make a bargain with Cinderella," she added, examining Cinderella's dress and jewelry.

"Why, you little thief!" Drizella cried. "Those are *my* beads!" And she snatched the necklace from Cinderella's neck.

"Look!" shrieked Anastasia. "That's my sash! She's wearing my sash!"

The two horrible girls ripped and tore and clawed at the dress. "Oh, stop, please!" begged Cinderella. She ran from the house to the garden, where she fell to her knees by a stone bench. She wept and wept.

"It's just no use," Cinderella said between sobs. "I can't believe in anything anymore. I can't believe in my dreams. There's nothing to believe in. Nothing."

"Nothing, my dear?"

"Oh, but I do mean it!" Cinderella insisted through her tears. Suddenly Cinderella realized a strange old woman had appeared in the garden.

"Nonsense, child!" the old woman said. "If you'd lost all your faith, I couldn't be here." She smiled kindly and gently lifted Cinderella to her feet. "Come now, dry those tears. You can't go to the ball looking like that."

"The ball?" Cinderella said. "Oh, but I'm not going."

"Of course you are," the old woman said matter-of-factly. "But we'll have to hurry, because even miracles take a little time."

In amazement Cinderella watched as her fairy godmother produced a wand out of the air.

"Now, the first thing you need is a pumpkin."

"A pumpkin?" Cinderella said.

"Ah," the old woman said, and then launched into the most peculiar song Cinderella had ever heard. It included such odd phrases as "bibbidi-bobbidi-boo" and "salaga-doola, menchicka-boola." It seemed difficult to believe that such nonsense would work magic, but with a wave of the fairy godmother's wand, Cinderella watched an ordinary pumpkin transform into a splendid coach.

"It's beautiful!" marveled Cinderella.

"Yes, it is, isn't it?" replied her fairy godmother. With the same magical touch of the wand, she then turned Gus, Jaq, and two other chateau mice into stately horses. An ordinary horse became a smart-looking coachman, and the dog a proper footman.

Grasping the wand, her fairy godmother waved it in the air until Cinderella was encircled by a spiral of light. Tiny stars winked along each ring, gaining in brilliance. Within moments an exquisite dress replaced the tattered rags. "It's so beautiful!" cried Cinderella. Then she saw the glass slippers on her feet.

"It's like a dream," Cinderella said, "a wonderful dream come true." She strode over to the fountain, not shy about admiring her reflection in the water.

"It can't last forever," warned her fairy godmother. "You have only until midnight. Then the spell will be broken, and everything will be as it was before."

"Oh, I understand," Cinderella assured her. "It's more than I ever hoped for."

Her fairy godmother smiled, then nodded. "Bless you, my child," she said. Then she hurried Cinderella into the coach.

Cinderella was the last to arrive at the palace, and she hurried up the grand staircase alone. It was all so elegant and magnificent that Cinderella did not notice the handsome young man admiring her from across the ballroom. He walked over and bowed politely. Cinderella curtsied. He gently took her hand, kissed it, and asked her to dance.

They danced and danced and danced. Cinderella felt as if she were dancing on air. Everything was more wonderful than she could ever have imagined—the dress, the slippers, the exquisite coach and beautiful horses, and the most handsome and charming man she had ever met.

A dream come true, Cinderella thought; I hope I never wake up.

THE GLASS SLIPPER

Cinderella had just learned the most extraordinary news—the prince was in love! She gazed contentedly at her own reflection as she combed her hair in front of the mirror. Last night at the ball she had danced with a handsome stranger, and under a star-filled sky just before midnight they had kissed. It had been so beautiful, as beautiful as a dream. But just as her fairy god-

mother had predicted, the dream ended with the tolling of the bells at midnight. In her haste to flee the palace, Cinderella had lost one of her glass slippers.

Now news swept through the kingdom that the prince had instructed the grand duke to find the girl whose foot fit the glass slipper. The prince was determined to find her and make her his bride. Cinderella was dizzy with happiness. Oh, it cannot be, she thought. My handsome stranger is the prince himself! She reached reassuringly into the pocket of her tattered apron. There it was . . . the other glass slipper. So it wasn't a dream after all, she thought happily.

Cinderella caught her reflection in the mirror at last. She was smiling. She could not remember any time in her life when she was happier. An excited chattering distracted her. Gus and Jaq had climbed onto the dresser and were hopping up and down.

"What is it?" Cinderella asked. "I can't understand you." Just then Cinderella saw in her mirror the grim face of her stepmother. The smile instantly slid from Cinderella's face. Lady Tremaine had one hand on the doorknob. In the other hand she dangled a key. The horrible woman meant to lock Cinderella away!

"No!" cried Cinderella, running to the door. But it was too late. The heavy door swung shut. Cinderella pulled at it helplessly. "Please," Cinderella begged. "Oh, please don't do this. Let me out!"

Tears sprang into Cinderella's eyes. Throwing herself to the floor, she began to sob. It's all so unfair, she thought to herself. Just then the clattering of carriage wheels on the cobblestones drew Cinderella to her window. A fancy carriage pulled up in front, and Cinderella recognized the man who alighted as the grand duke.

"Here I am!" Cinderella called from high up in her garret, but her cries floated away like so many leaves in the wind. Cinderella was in despair. Whatever was she to do!

Never lose faith, her fairy godmother had said. Very well, Cinderella decided. I will remain strong. I must escape. Cinderella examined her room. Certainly she was too high up to climb out the window. Therefore, the door was her only means of escape. Cinderella braced herself and pulled at the doorknob with all her strength. She pulled and pulled until she could pull no longer and fell exhausted to the floor. "Oh, it's all no use," she moaned. The door would not budge. Cinderella fell to her knees and wept.

A strange noise on the other side of the door drew Cinderella to her knees. Peering through the keyhole, she could scarcely believe her eyes. Gus and Jaq! And a key!

"How did you ever manage?" Cinderella cried out with delight. Then Cinderella saw something that filled her with terror—Lucifer, her stepmother's cat. Lucifer pounced on Gus and trapped him under an overturned cereal bowl.

"Lucifer! Let him go!" Cinderella said severely. Lucifer ignored her with a smug swish of his tail. "Quickly," Cinderella called out to her other friends, the birds. "Find Bruno." And before long Cinderella could hear Bruno's familiar barking. Up the stairs came Bruno in an excited dash, and when he caught sight of Lucifer, he sent up a bloodcurdling howl. The poor cat leapt up as if struck by lightning. Cinderella had to laugh. So often she had scolded Bruno for being so mean to Lucifer. But not today, she thought with relief.

The chateau mice quickly managed to slide the key under the door. Cinderella let herself out, thanked her friends, and rushed downstairs.

"Your Grace!" Cinderella called out. The grand duke had already put on his hat when Cinderella came dashing into the room. Breathlessly Cinderella asked, "May I please try on the slipper?"

Lady Tremaine hastily stepped in front of Cinderella. "Pay no at-

tention to her, Your Grace," she said in an apologetic tone.

"It is only our scullery maid," Drizella and Anastasia said.

The grand duke took Cinderella by the hand and led her to a chair. He motioned for his footman to bring the slipper. Not about to see either of her daughters cheated of a chance to marry a prince, however, Lady Tremaine set her cane in the path of the footman. He stumbled, and the glass slipper crashed to the floor.

"Now what is to be done?" the grand duke moaned. The footman fell to his knees and tried to gather together the shattered remains of the slipper. It was no use. Across Lady Tremaine's face came a grin of deep satisfaction.

The grand duke was not amused.

"I have the other slipper," Cinderella said.

Lady Tremaine gasped. The grand duke stared at Cinderella in disbelief. His eyes followed her hand to the pocket of her tattered apron. He smiled as she withdrew the slipper.

Lady Tremaine turned pale. Anastasia and Drizella looked as if they might faint. The grand duke took the slipper and gently slipped it onto Cinderella's foot. It glittered in the light like a thousand diamonds.

Taking Cinderella's hand, the grand duke led her away from the cottage to the carriage that waited out front — a carriage that would carry her to her dream.

Beyond the Palace Walls

It's just no fun being a princess.
I can't even choose my own mate.
They think I should marry a prince in three days.
Too bad—I shall make them all wait!

I'm sick and tired of prince after prince—
Every last one is a bore,
Yet here comes another arrogant fool,
Marching his way through the door!

I'd much rather sit by the fountain
And be free from this royal duty—
How many more suitors must I hear
Boast of their wealth and their beauty?

I've never been outside the palace walls.
I'm feeling a little bit trapped.
If I could escape to the world just outside,
As a commoner I could adapt.

And maybe, just maybe, I might meet a boy,
A companion who's clever and kind.
Together we'd share an adventurous life,
And he'd let me make up my own mind!

Aladdin

THE BOY IN THE MARKETPLACE

Princess Jasmine expected her father in the garden at any moment. She had rejected yet another suitor, this time the overdressed, self-absorbed Prince Achmed.

Sure enough, the sultan confronted her. "Dearest," he said, "you've got to stop rejecting every suitor who comes to call. The law says you must be married to a prince by your next birthday."

"The law is wrong," protested Jasmine.

"You've got only three more days!"

The princess loved her father dearly, but she did not understand his insistence on following such ancient, outdated laws. She strolled over to the large ornate cage that housed her collection of birds. She opened the door and took one out. She stroked its soft feathers. I wish I could be somewhere else, she thought — rather than repeating the same argument with her kind, but misguided, father.

"Father," Jasmine explained for what seemed the millionth time, "I hate being forced into this. If I do marry, I want it to be for love."

The sultan was growing impatient. "Jasmine, it's not only the law. I'm not going to be around forever, and . . . well, I just want to make sure you're taken care of. Provided for." He gently took the bird from her hand and placed it back in its cage.

Jasmine wandered over to a fountain. "Please try to understand,

Father. I've never done a thing on my own. I've never had any real friends except Rajah. I've never even been outside the palace walls!"

"But Jasmine, you're a princess!"

Jasmine shot her father a defiant glance. "Then maybe I don't want to be a princess anymore!" She splashed her hand in the fountain, spoiling her reflection.

Having had his patience exhausted once again, the sultan flung his hands into the air and stormed back to the throne room. "Oooh, Allah forbid you should have any daughters!" he complained to Rajah. Rajah blinked uncomprehendingly, but Jasmine understood what her father meant.

She strolled back to the menagerie and watched the birds in their cages. I wonder what it's like to be free, she thought. Suddenly Jasmine threw open the doors to the birdcages. "Fly away!" Jasmine called to them. It was thrilling to watch the birds soar over the palace, heading for. . . . Jasmine shook her head sadly. Heading for anywhere but here, she thought. And then she had an idea. Jasmine found an old cloak and prepared to climb over the palace wall. As she clambered up a tree, she felt something tug on her leg. It was Rajah, trying to hold her back.

"I'm sorry, Rajah," she explained. "But I can't stay here and have my life lived for me. I'll miss you."

The tiger let go of her cloak. "Good-bye," she said. Then she climbed over the wall and disappeared.

The city of Agrabah delighted Jasmine. The marketplace, with its crush of people and carts, was especially thrilling. As she wandered through the crowd, Jasmine watched fruit sellers and fishmongers and rug merchants hawking their wares. She gaped at a sword swallower and inhaled pungent spices and fragrant perfumes. Even the

noisy clatter of people arguing and gossiping made her pause and listen.

It's all so wonderful, Jasmine thought. Wonderful and alive!

Jasmine was distracted by a ragged little boy who stood gazing desperately at an apple in front of a fruit seller's cart. "You must be hungry," she said, plucking the apple from the cart. "Here you go." The child grabbed the apple and dashed into the crowd. Smiling, Jasmine watched him go. Then she felt someone grab her arm roughly.

"You'd better be able to pay for that," said the angry fruit seller. Jasmine was confused. As a princess from the palace, she had no need of money. The vendor leaned closer. "No one steals from *my* cart," he snarled.

"I'm sorry, sir," Jasmine replied. "I don't have any money."

"Then you're a thief!"

The fruit seller tightened his grip. "Please," she pleaded, "if you let me go to the palace, I can get some money from the sultan."

The vendor sneered and held a knife over her fingers. "Do you know what the penalty is for stealing?" he asked. Suddenly his arm was pulled back.

"Thank you, kind sir," said a stranger with what seemed to be immense relief. The vendor eyed him warily. "I'm so glad you found her." The boy turned to Jasmine. "I've been looking all over for you!" The boy winked at her.

"What are you doing?" Jasmine whispered frantically.

"Just play along!" the boy muttered.

"You know this girl?" the fruit seller demanded.

The boy sighed tragically.

"Sadly, yes, she is my sister." He motioned with his hand to his

head. "She's just a little crazy," he tried to explain.

"Your sister said she knew the sultan," the vendor said.

The boy pointed to his pet monkey, Abu. "She thinks the *monkey* is the sultan," he replied.

Jasmine bowed to the monkey. "O Wise Sultan," she said, playing along, "how may I serve you?"

Abu sat up importantly and patted Jasmine on the head. The vendor scowled, but the crowd roared with laughter. The boy sneaked an apple from the cart and handed it to the fruit seller. "No harm done," he said. "Now, come along, sis. Time to go see the doctor."

Jasmine followed the boy obediently but paused in front of a camel. "Hello, Doctor, how are you?" she said, and bowed courteously. Again the crowd erupted into gales of laughter.

At that moment Abu dropped an armload of apples he had swiped. "Come back here, you little thieves!" the vendor shouted.

"Quick!" the boy shouted. He took Jasmine by the hand. "Follow me!"

They fled through the streets of the marketplace, up one alley and down another. Jasmine was amazed at herself for trusting this fast-talking stranger. Still, she conceded to herself, he *did* rescue me from the fruit seller.

The boy helped Jasmine climb onto a rooftop. "This is your first time in the marketplace, isn't it?" he asked finally.

Jasmine laughed. "Is it that obvious?"

"Well, you do kind of stand out. I mean, you don't seem to know how dangerous Agrabah can be." He took Jasmine's hand and led her to a torn curtain and a makeshift hammock.

"Is this where you live?" asked Jasmine.

"Yes. Just me and Abu. We come and go as we please."

"That sounds fabulous," Jasmine said enviously.

"Well, it's not much, but it's got a great view." The boy pulled aside the shabby curtain. In the distance the walls of the palace glowed in the setting sun.

"Wow, the palace looks pretty amazing, doesn't it?" he asked.

"Oh, it's wonderful," Jasmine replied blandly.

"I wonder what it would be like to live there and have servants and valets."

"Sure," said Jasmine wearily. "People who tell you where to go and how to dress."

"It's better than this place. You're always scraping for food and ducking the guards."

The boy took one of the stolen apples and tossed it to Jasmine.

"So where are you from?" he asked.

"Does it matter?" Jasmine said. "I ran away, and I'm not going back."

"Really?" he asked. "How come?"

"My father is forcing me to get married."

"That's awful," he declared.

As the two talked, Jasmine found herself staring into the boy's eyes. I *should* be afraid of him, she thought. But there is something about him that makes me feel safe. Perhaps he felt it, too, because suddenly their faces were close enough to kiss.

"Here you are!" shouted a soldier who appeared at the edge of the rooftop.

"They're after me!" Jasmine and the boy shouted at the same time. They stared at each other in confusion. The soldiers came toward them. The boy took a quick look over the edge of the roof. He turned to Jasmine.

"Do you trust me?" he asked. Again Jasmine peered into his eyes.
"Yes," she said.

"Then jump!"

Together Jasmine and the boy climbed onto the terrace wall and jumped.

One of the sultan's soldiers was waiting for them beside the pile of hay on the street below.

"It's the dungeon for you, boy!" the soldier growled.

Jasmine blocked his path. "Unhand him by order of the princess!" she demanded. The soldier scoffed and pushed her roughly to the ground. The hood of the cloak that shielded her face fell away, and the soldier gasped.

"Princess Jasmine! What are you doing outside the palace? And with this street rat?"

Jasmine was furious. "That's not your concern. Do as I command. Release him."

The soldier shrugged. His orders to arrest this street urchin had come from Jafar, the vizier to the sultan, he explained.

There was nothing she could do. Jasmine watched helplessly as the boy was dragged away to the dungeon. It isn't fair! Jasmine thought angrily. She remembered with contempt her horrible afternoon with the arrogant Prince Achmed. He could think of nothing but himself. This boy, on the other hand, who had nothing at all—not even a decent home or enough food to eat—had risked everything to save *her*.

"I'll go to Jafar!" she promised. "I will have him released."

On the orders of Jafar, however, the boy had already been sentenced to death. Princess Jasmine wept and wept.

"I didn't even know his name!"

THE MAGIC CARPET RIDE

*A*grabah was dazzled by the arrival of the fabulous Prince Ali Ababwa—everyone, that is, but Princess Jasmine.

From her balcony at the palace, Jasmine watched the prince's lavish parade with fascination and contempt. How garish and extreme, she told herself. Even the prince's menagerie disappointed her. His collection of exotic creatures seemed designed only to impress. Jasmine assumed with weary resignation that Prince Ali Ababwa was yet another suitor chosen by her father.

Jasmine left the balcony and wandered into the garden. How arrogant and pompous they are, Jasmine thought, remembering her parade of suitors. She frowned. There is no reason why I should have to wait for a prince to be introduced to me. *I* should march into the throne room and introduce *myself.*

In the throne room a young man was speaking to her father and Jafar. "Your Majesty," the young man said. "I am Prince Ali Ababwa! Just let her meet me. I will win your daughter!"

Jasmine was enraged. "How dare you!" she shouted. "All of you! Standing around, deciding my future. I am not a prize to be won!"

She turned and ran to her room. "Prince Ali Ababwa!" she sneered. "His arrogance is the worst yet!"

That evening Jasmine walked onto her balcony. The lights of the city of Agrabah twinkled like stars in the dusk. Jasmine could not help thinking about the young man in the marketplace.

The city had never looked as beautiful as when she had stood with him on the terrace that late afternoon. Our faces were close enough to kiss, she recalled with a mixture of joy and sorrow.

Jasmine strolled inside. From the balcony came a voice. "Princess Jasmine? It's me, Prince Ali Ababwa."

"I do not want to see you!" she exclaimed.

"No, please, Princess," he begged. "Give me a chance."

Jasmine peered at the figure in the dim light. "Wait—do I know you?"

"Uh, no," he said.

Jasmine sighed. "You remind me of someone I met in the marketplace. . . ."

"The marketplace?" The prince laughed nervously. "I have servants who go to the marketplace for me. Why, I have servants who go to the marketplace for my servants. So it couldn't have been me you met."

"No, I guess not," she said.

Jasmine heard the prince mumble something about her "being beautiful." Jasmine had grown weary of being admired only for her looks and wealth. She decided to test this newest suitor. "I'm rich, too, you know," she said.

"Yeah." He sounds impressed, Jasmine said to herself.

She stepped closer. "I'm the daughter of a sultan."

"I know," he murmured. Oooh, the rascal, Jasmine thought.

"A fine prize for any prince to marry."

"Right," smiled the prince. "A prince like me."

"Right!" Jasmine shouted scornfully. "A prince like you and every other stuffed-shirt, swaggering peacock I've met. Go jump off a balcony!"

"You're right," the prince conceded. "You aren't just some prize to be won. You should be free to make your own choice."

Jasmine watched Prince Ali step off the balcony.

"No!" she cried. Instead of falling, the prince stood as if on air.

"How are you doing that?" she asked. Calmly the prince rose into the air on a beautifully colored magic carpet.

"It's lovely," Jasmine said.

"You don't want to go for a ride, do you?" Prince Ali asked. "We could get out of the palace, see the world."

"Is it safe?" she asked.

"Sure. Do you trust me?"

Jasmine stared dumbfounded. "What?" she asked.

"Do you trust me?" Prince Ali repeated. Could it be? she wondered.

"Yes," Jasmine replied, taking his hand.

The prince pulled her onto the carpet. It was like sailing on the wind! Jasmine gazed down and saw the lights of Agrabah blaze, then disappear. Ahead, the moonlit desert lay silent and empty.

It was like no magic Jasmine had ever known.

From Arabia they soared past the pyramids of Egypt. Jasmine was seeing things she had seen only in books or learned from her tutor. For only the second time in her life, Jasmine had journeyed beyond the palace walls.

"It's all so . . . magical," Jasmine said.

"Yeah," Prince Ali agreed.

"It's a shame Abu had to miss this," she remarked casually.

"Nah," said the prince. "He doesn't really like—" Prince Ali stopped in midsentence. "Ah, that is—," he stumbled.

"You *are* the boy from the marketplace!" Jasmine exclaimed. "Why did you lie to me?" she demanded angrily.

"Jasmine, I'm sorry."

"Did you think I was stupid? Did you think that I wouldn't figure it out?"

"No," he blurted. "I mean, I hoped you wouldn't. No, that's not what I meant."

Jasmine faced him. "Who are you really? Tell me the truth."

"The truth? The truth?" he said. "The truth is that I sometimes dress as a commoner, to escape the pressures of palace life. But I really am a prince."

Jasmine understood all too well the prince's need to escape. After all, she had tried to run away once herself.

"Why didn't you just tell me?" she asked.

"Well, you know, royalty going out into the city in disguise—it sounds a little strange, don't you think?"

Actually, Jasmine didn't think it sounded strange in the least. How often she had dreamed about being someone else, someone who was free to roam wherever she pleased and to do whatever she liked. She wanted to ask Ali how he had avoided being beheaded by Jafar, but she did not want to spoil the mood. There will be time enough, she thought.

The evening had been so beautiful that Jasmine was reluctant to have it end. But it was late, she realized. And she must return.

Prince Ali gave the order to his magic carpet, and all too soon Jasmine saw the twinkling lights of Agrabah in the distance. The magic carpet ride was over.

Ali helped Jasmine off the magic carpet and onto her balcony. They bumped lightly into one another and for a long moment stared into each other's eyes. Then they kissed.

"Good night, my handsome prince," Jasmine whispered before she turned and went inside to dream of her newfound love.

J